I0819966

For my baby brother, Chris.

WHISPER

A PRELUDE TO NECROMANTICA

A novelette by Keith Blenman

Blue Donut Books

ISBN: 978-0-578-50909-9

Speak of Me

Speak of me as if I were dead.
I will return to you with the same honor.
Speak to me as if I were gone.
Passed away from your effect. Beyond your reach.
Send out your words as if you doubt I will ever hear them.
As if you know I will never reply.

Test the waters of reflection knowing you swim with only your own ripples.
Rings of energy running away.
I will pay the same respect upon seeing your face.

-Thomas Budday

WHISPER

Arise, Lector.

Arise, Lector.

"I cannot."

Arise, Lector. Open your eyes.

"Butterscotch is making her nest. If I move she'll panic. If I move I'll destroy her home."

Arise, Lector. Your daughter is in danger.

"But who will keep Butterscotch warm?"

She'll be fine. Through you I feel her heartbeat. I feel her pups. Three are kicking.

"They're made of me, you know. Her, her mouse husband, and me. When she eats my flesh I feel it pass through her, nourishing her pups. Flecks of myself become her babies, become alive again. Unborn. Flecks of myself exist within her. She lives in my heart. I live within hers. Don't you see?"

That's lovely, Lector. But there's no time. Only noble blood can pass the seal. Your daughter is in danger and you must save her. Now open your eyes.

The seal? The amber seal of Gralt? Laid by my dwarven ancestors and enchanted by the wizards of old, only the blood of my family and those invited may pass the third floor of the keep. All others perish. Should my bloodline end they say the seal will shatter, bringing down the entire castle, the mountain, and the mines within.

As a boy I used to attempt to leap over the seal. That is until I saw a Fortian man –some eager and naive messenger- attempt to pass it. "I bring glad tidings from the true king!" he'd said while gleefully pushing his way past the guards. As though news from the pure kingdom meant anything beyond some ploy. Two steps over the seal had been as far as he was allowed. Two steps and he became engulfed in azure flames. All watched as he dissipated into a cloud of ash, the echo of his scream still lingering through the hall. My father chuckled. As did the guards. I saw magic for the first time and with it the joy in taking a leap had passed.

Yes, Lector. You remember the sacred seal. What of your daughter? Do you remember Alaila?

Alaila? The name pulses with guilt although I know not why. I think on a girl, almost a woman. Always quiet and passive. There is little dwarf in her. "Yes!" I say. "I spoke of her many times to my darling Clea." My little girl, Alaila. She was born under the thirteenth night of five moons. I feared for her. She was too malleable, moved too easy to tears. I sent her away. Somewhere. To Fortia, I think. I made her the voice of the mountain in hope that she might learn her strength.

"You'll speak for your people," I had told her, looking out a window to the village Ara. It was mid morning, I think. I remember the warmth of the sun. I remember warmth. I remember pointing to the rooftop gardens, the silver-bricked homes, and thousands of miners on their early march to cave entrance beneath the castle. "Fortians have become corrupt with their own grace. They are a vile people, living for the heavens and not the earth. You cannot know how many they've slaughtered as heathens. All in what they called a purification. And yet we'd be unable to trade with half the world if not for safe passage through their wilds. They cannot risk war for fear of our allies, but with our wealth they could conquer the world. They know this as well as I. You must appeal to their pride. Make King Stolzel glad for our alliance. But never allow them an inch they don't deserve."

She'd nodded, but said nothing. As a princess and my only heir she should've been honored. It was more than her duty. It was her right. Yet as we looked upon the mountainside I knew all I had robbed from her. I cast her from paradise to dwell among the beasts.

Yes. Alaila. That's right. Now open your eyes.

I do as the whisper commands. Inches overhead I see my family crest. The crescent of a single moon arches over a mink, etched in rock from the Caves of Ara. In dwarfish it reads, "Rest Here Protector of Stone." I'm within the Crypt of Lords, lying in my coffin.

Can you move? the whisper asks from some distant nowhere inside my mind. *I can move for you if you can't. But it's easier if you try with me.*

The skin of my hands rips at the joints as I stretch my fingers. I feel every crick and pop surge through my weathered bones. It's agonizing. But distant. The trauma tears me. It echoes the hurt in an alarm of throbbing pulses. And yet I feel removed.

It's as though some reflection of myself is writhing in agony. I know the pain but only watch it. Within me I feel Butterscotch stir to the tremors of my cracking joints. Her paws press against the walls of my heart, scraping as she steadies herself. Her world just moved and she fears for her litter.

Good. Now lift the lid. You can't save Alaila from a coffin.

I don't understand. Something wicked weaves from the voice in my head. I resist but the whisper won't have it. Chills prickle my arms and cause my elbows to jerk. My knuckles grind against the stone, grating flakes of flesh into the grooves of the family crest.

Now push.

I press my fists into the stone and the chill thrashes from my shoulders to my knuckles. I push. The whisper pushes through me. Together we slide several hundred pounds of rock enough to force an opening. Without my control, my hands graze along the edges. My feet shift within the coffin, slipping against their confinement. Inside my chest Butterscotch is digging her paws. She fights for stable ground. Her heart races, waking the pups and making them squirm.

"How are you doing this?" I ask as my body hoists itself from the coffin. I know this room. I'm within the deepest nook of the crypt. The place itself, formed within a vein of galena was hollowed by my dwarven ancestors and refined to its silver luster. I've been here before and all the quiet memories come creeping back. I used to sit below on a marble bench and confide to the graves of my elders. I spoke of my woes. My triumphs. I pleaded for the strength to rule justly from those who had come before. Never did they answer, but through them I found my metal. All my life I had known I would some day join them. Never did I imagine to actually see it. But twisting my way from my coffin, I know precisely where I am. Above me rests Korsk, The Lord Reclaimer, and his wife, Vimela. My father and mother. Above them are my great grandparents, Lector the Fifth and Bruemmie, the first pure human couple of my lineage in several generations.

Why do you not recall the graves of your grandparents?

"The outcasts?" I say. "We do not speak of those who lost our lands. They did not keep the earth. They hold no place within it."

I feel your wrath. Good.

I feel sadness. Confusion. Feelings I cannot rightfully claim in regards to my ancestors. "Are these yours?" I ask the whisper. It lifts my body from the coffin and rolls me to the vacant space alongside it. Space meant for and thankfully unoccupied by my darling Clea. "These tormented pains? Are they yours?"

As my body twists over itself the whisper sighs and an echo of mourning rattles through my mind. *The feelings are my own*, it says. *We are joined. I can see within you, manipulate you. The price is that we bleed onto each other. But fear not. I'll be gone once the task is complete.*

The whisper urges me to crawl to the lip of my alcove. I gaze out on the soft luster of the crypt. Although no light shines I'm able to see its gleam. Fifty rows of shelves encircling my family crest with a wide ring of benches on the floor below. From the fourth highest row I look down upon the generations of Ara. At its lowest levels, the coffins are suited best for dwarves. But as the years passed and unions with human folk became more common, the alcoves were dug deeper. For several generations dwarves were entombed in coffins fit for men. Over time the human breeding won out. At present we looked neither human nor dwarf but somewhere between. Tough as the rocks, lean as the picks. That is the only proper way to describe the house of Ara. A house I had been protector of all my life. That is, after my father had reclaimed it and passed its glory on to me. A life cut short, it would seem. "Do you see through me as well," I ask the whisper. "As I look upon the resting places of my kin do you learn their stories?"

I do. Whitrik the Diamond Back, who was pummeled by goblin hammers until they exhausted themselves. He then cleaved them all with his axe. Far to the side is Vrunt, who was an especially well loved diplomat among the elves. The first to take a human wife I believe. And then there's Flynt Carrot Chaser, leader of the war pony brigade. Beneath him is Bruger Stout Head, who you know little of.

"The name means something to you though. I feel a discomfort at the thought of him. Not that Bruger, but another. I sense adoration. Love. And agony. Did you love a dwarf?" The whisper says nothing, but instead inches my body so that my arms hang freely over the ledge. "Forgive my asking," I say. "I sense your discomfort. And you're right. We have a long descent ahead of us."

I think not.

The whisper urges me forward. Rather than reaching for another alcove or handhold, the chill flows from my limbs and collects within my chest. I can acquaint the sensation to restoring feeling after numbness but I continue to lack any means of control.

My body spills from its shelf and drops to the crest below. “Butterscotch!” I screamed, but am helpless to shield the mouse from the fall. My head and shoulder slap helplessly against the galena floor. The rest of me rolls over itself into a heap of crossed and contorted limbs. The impact rattles my bones. Some even fracture. And yet I feel nothing. My wits are scattered. Nothing more. A wave of ease crests over me when I feel the little heartbeat within my own. The cave mouse is fine. Frightened but safe. The pups within her flail and writhe about their sacks, but the mother makes no effort to retreat. She is within her home. Whatever horror it is that takes place outside my walls, she feels secure from.

You're a good man, Lector, to worry over helpless creatures.

“Reckless, insolent voice!” I say. “I know not whether to be more disturbed by the part of you that plays with a corpse or the part that carelessly gambles with the lives of innocent mice.”

Calm down, Lector. The chill leaves my chest and rolls through my limbs. I feel portions of muscles within me rip at their lowest layers. They slither in places, coiling around joints and asphyxiating my fractures. My most rotted places tighten and enforce themselves. *Your body was well preserved and your organs are soft. I too could never hurt such innocent creatures. Do not fear. Mice can manage such falls without your heart to cushion them. Within you they are safer still. So calm yourself. We need to move.*

The chill surges through my entirety. Pins prickle, making my body shiver to its knees. It lifts from the ground, standing, stumbling its way to both feet. I pat my chest, lightly feeling for the movement within. Some faint tremors, nothing that resembles my own heart. Just a mouse in its den protecting her unborn children. And then a thought occurs. It was not the whisper but I who moved my arm. "How is this possible?" I ask, freely examining the tattered flesh of my fingers. "How are you doing this?"

I'm able to. It takes considerable concentration, but if I focus I can allow you some measure of control. You will feel more alive and able to act as such. You know this castle, Lord Lector Ara. It will be easier for us both if you're able to reach your daughter without my manipulation of your every gesture.

"What magic is this? What are you?" The whisper says nothing, but somewhere deep within I feel the sway of trees and scorch of fire. I see butterflies incinerated. I see wood elves scattered then petrified. I feel a hole as deep as the night sky and all of it filled with blood. And then I feel my legs step out of the crypt.

I am like you, the whisper says with daggers of admonition. Whatever memories I found cease at an instant.

"Am I not a corpse?" I ask. "Do you fear I'll share your secrets between the moons and The Black?"

The Black knows my secrets. I wish not to think on them myself.

Together in my body we ascend through the catacombs. Dwarven and human families are all buried in these layers, all of them gathered in crypts akin to my own. Some cousins. Some brothers. Others of dear friends and their families. Some dusty crypts belong to the unvisited families who died out ages ago. Crypts upon crypts, branching deeper and deeper into the earth. Old mines, they were once. The families, the community, all together we harvested these rocks. We reaped the precious gems and secured our place in the world. The furthest, deepest holes extend into mines, still pulling silver to this day. Every morning the workers of Ara pass their heritage before continuing onward. Every night they return home and thank their ancestors for allowing them to continue in their tradition. For all of us together brought the beauty of the world to its surface. We lived by the earth. We died and returned ourselves to it. That is the way. The mines are life beneath the tombs.

I stagger through generations, rising to the surface. Butterscotch's claws ease as I make my way. My slow, dragging movements calm her young and allow them all to drift themselves to slumber. "The mines are empty," I note as I reach a main passage. "Even at night there is always some activity at this depth."

The people of your banner are both in mourning and resting themselves for celebration. Your daughter is sentenced to marriage tomorrow.

"Marriage? How long have I been dead?"

Not yet four weeks.

I lose my step and begin to crumble, but the whisper runs its will and urges me onward. "Four weeks? Alaila was not engaged at my passing. I hadn't even allowed her audience with suitors. She's too young to rule. Why has Clea allowed this?"

Your wife has taken ill since your passing, Lector. Fear not though. I'm certain she'll return to good health once the ceremony is over. She rests until then.

I do not care for the whisper's ominous tone. It suspects treachery, but withholds enough to let my imagination drift. It thinks over a sleeping poison. I wish to know more but the whisper turns its thoughts to my legs. Through it I feel a stirring of both anger and betrayal.

I reach the adit of the mines and take comfort to find myself surrounded by the familiar walls of my palace. Stories over the rest of the village, the castle stands as a singular trunk tower, spanning from the peak of Mount Grumich and stretching well into the moonlight. At its crest, the tower branches into a number of offshoots. Within they hold the homes of the noble family and offices of government. Outsiders from Fortia and other nations dubbed it Castle Tree Top. And it was inspiration from that name that led my great, great dwarven grandfather to adorn the uppermost levels with a crusting of emeralds. From every horizon Castle Tree Top glimmers to be admired. It is the symbol of life and prosperity for all who live under its embrace. Of course the locals have another name for it. The villagers and miners living on the mountainside refer to it more properly as Castle Ara. As for myself and my kin, we've always known it as home.

I feel Butterscotch adjust herself into ball. She rests her head on a single paw and breathes a slow rhythm against my heart. A gentle accent to the quiet comfort of night.

Go to the armory. You'll require a weapon.

I do as the whisper commands. With the mine entrance at the center of the castle's keep, the armory is immediately beside it. Should any enemy come from outside or tunneled through below, the guards of Ara are ready. Not that any threat has entered my lands since my father reclaimed the castle from the defilers. The wizards who bribed my family off the mountain were punished for their crimes. My grandparents were made to suffer along with them. But even that last true display of violence ended in condemnation. Not death. While often our lands are placed under the threat of corruption, combat is a rare misfortune. The mountain range proves too narrow and difficult for a direct assault. Spies and scouts alike are spotted well before approaching the village. With even minimal defenses, we are safe from the outside world. Still, no fool would leave a place of infinite treasure unguarded.

You think this. Future generations may wish to enhance their combat skills.

I find the armory's main door ajar. Stepping within I see five dwarven soldiers unconscious the floor. Each of them is bound and gagged. My compulsion is to raise an alarm, but I can feel the whisper laugh over my surprise. "You did this?" I ask.

My companion opened the way for you.

"Companion?"

As I said. You'll require a weapon.

The whisper gives me little choice but to step over my former guards. I look upon them as I pass, remembering each of them. Pug, who bred enough dogs to earn such a name. Clarth and Yastol, who together forged many of the mountain's shovels and picks. Quimkkol, the commander of the guard and my royal advisor. I'm compelled to unbind his hands, but the whisper continues its push. At least until we both notice the last of my men breathing heavily through his gag. The whisper and I can't help but take in the wide whites of his eyes.

This one is awake, the whisper says in its distant echo. *It seems my companion was lax in his effort.*

"His name is Mrack," I say. "A father of three. He whittles children's toys and games in the evenings. And your companion left quite a bruising on his face." I step toward the guard and he tries to scream through his gag. The chill eases, allowing me to raise my open hands and kneel before him.

Did you know all the men of your kingdom by name?

"I was their Lord," I say. "What sort of man rules over another without learning his name?" I place a rotted hand on Mrack's shoulder and let his screams quiet back down to heaving breaths. He writhes another moment but settles into glaring at me, shivering. "He didn't deserve to be injured this way. He is a good man."

He is a soldier. It was necessary. You require a weapon. If he saw you unbound he'd attack you.

I cannot argue the whisper. Thoughts form, but are dampened. It knows my argument and wishes not to hear it. For a moment I fear it aims to have me murder the man. Instead the chill surges through me and forces me to stand.

Come along. We'll leave him to speak of your deeds in the morning.

As I enter the weapon cache, a creeping movement catches my eye. Both the whisper and I turn to face some putrid, withered creature. It is a horrid, jawless waste of marbled flesh dripping over bones. To say my reflection is unsettling is a generous sentiment.

Forgive me, the whisper sighs. *Had I known I would've manipulated you into not seeing yourself.*

"So this is death?" I say, approaching the sight of my remains. Within me I feel Butterscotch roll to her side and stretch. Through the mirror I see a lump form from her feet betwixt two of my ribs. Even in darkness, it pains to see how much of me I've lost. In my middle age I'd developed a full, dwarven belly. Years in the mines had made boulders of my arms. Now I can watch my bones roll in their joints. "Butterscotch must've eaten more of my innards than I'd thought," I say. A patch of my flesh had been gashed open beneath my collar bone. At first I think it the result of several weeks' stay in a coffin. But as I inspect the reflection of the wound I make out a series of cuts and slices. Stitched triplets of gashes run over the whole of me. Above, I can see the column of my neck, and what I assume is my tongue protruding from an open flap of esophagus. "Where is my jaw?" I say.

That is no tongue. And your assassin was required by contract to bring your beard as evidence for his payment. With his swords, he found it timelier to cleave your mouth than shave you.

"My assassin?"

You do not recall your death?

I do not. I know I had passed. All this time I could feel my body fading and Butterscotch taking what she needed for her pups. But I was distant. Somewhere else. I know not where. Nearly gone until the whisper had summoned me.

You were in a hunting party. In the Western wilds. It was meant to look as though you happened upon a bear. It seems your killer graced you with a soft death and then staged your body after.

Some fluid must've poured out my eyes and rolled left, staining a mask-like spatter across my face. All that remained were two hollow sockets. Deep within them I can see a soft, green glow. "My bastard killer took my eyes as well?"

You no longer require sight in death so the world reclaims them. The glow is me. Or rather a result of me. As long as we are linked I see through you. Forgive my staring, but I notice your skin to the left is purple. Stained from the blood you hadn't lost in death.

"Yes. People of Ara are buried on their side. Even in death we do not lie on our backs."

I gaze at the horror I've become until it overwhelms. The thought creeps in that Mrack saw me this way. His king. His friend. Rotted and putrid. Every memory of me will be overshadowed with the nightmare the whisper and I gave him.

You require a weapon.

"Would you grant me some dignity first?"

The whisper says nothing, but its chill directs me to raid the guards' wardrobe. I'm quick to mask my face with a winter shawl. Leather slacks conceal my twiggy legs, and with a belt I'm able to fasten them over my hip bones. I place a scale mail over my chest, which rattles loosely over my vacant torso. Thick gloves give the illusion of strong hands. Steel topped boots create sturdy feet. In my reflection I can see a figure closer resembling myself.

"This assassin," I say to the whisper, although it begins to sink in that I'm not speaking at all. "Is he the one set on killing my daughter?" I peruse the battle axes, seeking a weapon suited for protecting my daughter.

He is. Take a sword.

The whisper's chill compels me to great swords racked on the opposing wall. Although I had been trained with such blades in my youth, I always favored axes and maces. I resist the urge, but it does me little good.

I'm better with a sword, it boasts. My arms are forced to pick up a two handed blade as tall as me. I could barely handle such a weapon in life. Swords such as this are used for slaughtering bears and dragons. But somehow my rotted body lifts the weapon with ease. Much like the lid of my coffin, I find both my will and the whisper's grant me strength greater than my own. The whisper pulses several chills through me and my arms swing the blade several times over. Deep grooves are slashed through the floor, ceiling, and nearest wall as though the armory were made of nothing sturdier than cheese.

"Very well," I say. "A sword it is."

It was always to be a sword. Now come to the courtyard. Your path beyond is blocked.

I climb the stairs another two stories. This floor of the castle was designed as a garden with the community in mind. The stone flooring is carpeted in a layer of soil and grass. Ornamenting the far walls are two fountains that spill an unending stream of water into little canals. Together they irrigate the many flowers, vines, and shrubberies. On three sides of the courtyard, the castle walls are open and supported by pillars shaped into the dwarven lords of old. My ancestors. Steel shutters were designed to fold over the windows in case of attack, but the only use they've been given over the years is protection from the winter air.

As I peak my head into the courtyard I'm met by two curious sites. The first is an elf girl and hooded man, seated at a table at the courtyard's center. They stare at a checkered board between them, chatting casually over what appears to be a game of chess. Instead of traditional pieces they play with a collection of knives stabbed into the board. The hooded man moves the silver blades. The elf girl's pieces are of blackened metal. They seem content to themselves, ignoring the second peculiar sight. At the far edge of the courtyard stands a small regiment of eight men clad in red and black armor. The insignia of a falcon's claw is embossed on their chest plates. They are soldiers from Fortia.

You see the problem? the whisper says, and the chill urges me to focus on the soldiers.

"What perversion allowed these men in my castle?" I say, although the answer comes clear as I form the question. I was assassinated and now my little Alaila is being forced to wed. It doesn't take much to realize a man of Fortia is meant to be her groom.

Hrathos Stolzel.

The Pure King's cousin. Again I'm overwhelmed and the whisper sends a chill to stand my ground. If my daughter marries a man from Fortia he will rule beside her and undoubtedly give my lands and people's riches to the holy kingdom. The moon worshippers. The pure blood humans. My hands tighten over the hilt of my sword. Not with any aid of the whisper.

Your people were rather displeased when Alaila returned for your funeral with news of an engagement. Some spat at her escort of Fortian soldiers. There was a small dispute, but with Fortia already in your walls there was little to be done. Your guards have mostly been disbanded. Your citizens held hostage, forced to play along in this coup-charade. Tomorrow there will be a wedding and by divine blessing of the moons, your banner will fly beneath Fortia's.

I stare up through the courtyard windows. Seeing the upper floors I can spot the window to my daughter's bed chamber. Not far from her is my wife's chamber, my chamber. The next branch over houses my brother, Djomc, and his heirs. Had I died from illness or age, I'd most certainly have named him as Ara's new lord. But with no such proclamation, the lands went to my daughter. "Why does Djomc not dispute Alaila?"

He has no claim and defying his lord is treason. He'd be outcast like your grandparents. Fortia is very well versed in your laws and traditions. You sent them your daughter. They knew exactly how to use her.

"So Hrathos has me murdered, forces my daughter into marriage, and then aims to kill her after the wedding. If I kill him, Fortia loses its chance to steal my lands." I say, entering the courtyard, convincing myself I'm ready for what must be done. The men ahead of me are Fortian. Enemies. I tell myself this as I tighten my grip on my sword. "What of the couple playing chess? Where do they fit in?"

The elf girl turns her head over her shoulder and stares at me. I'm stricken by her beauty in the moonlight. Pale, porcelain skin and black hair flowing down the entirety of her back. Her eyes, the same green shade that glows in my empty sockets. *We're here to see justice done*, the whisper says. Then she turns back to her chess partner. Plucking a blade from the board she says aloud, "I told you he was coming."

"Very well," her hooded partner says. "I am impressed. Your necromancy goes further than I'd imagined. But even if the guards don't hack him to pieces, he'll still be incinerated once he tries to pass the royal seal."

"Noble blood is noble blood," the elf says, stabbing her knife into a different portion of the board. "Besides, he's already passed the seal once in part. Check."

Her hooded companion plucks a knife and uses it to swat away the elf's game piece. He then thrusts his blade into the same space.

"Oy!" one of the Fortan soldier's screams, unsheathing a long sword and poising it in my direction. "Who goes there?"

To the whisper I ask, "What happens if they stab me? Or what if I'm beheaded?"

Fear not. I've handled this sort before.

The chill ripples through me and my legs pick up speed. "Wait," I say. "Wait. I need to let Butterscotch out first. Let me gouge myself. They'll aim for my heart. What if they hit Butterscotch?"

The whisper sends a feeling of calm, but says nothing. I hold the sword to my side with both hands as I step through the middle of the courtyard, closing in on the guards.

"You two," one of the guards screams to the chess players as he draws his sword. "Get out of here! Go home. It's no longer safe."

I continue my march forward, angling my arms to ready a swing.

The hooded man winks at the guard as he says, "It's only unsafe for you."

Several of the soldiers charge me. One raises his long sword over his head to strike but the whisper forces me to swing for him. Blood plumes everywhere as his arms are cleaved free at the elbows. His sword drops, grazing his scalp and slicing his ear.

He screams over an erratic flinch. Another quick slice gashes his throat and in the same motion parries the thrust of his nearest comrade. With his weapon deflected I crush his groin with the steel plate of my boot.

Another soldier runs in swinging. The chill urges me to step aside and slam against him with my shoulder. It's enough of a nudge that he trips over his own foot and collapses in a spiral.

Within me, Butterscotch begins to tussle. I feel her claws dig into me, again seeking stable ground.

I return to the guard I'd kicked. He's hunched on all fours with his head drooped low. By no means is he a threat but I sense the whisper cares little. Her chill surges and the sword swings down, splitting him between the shoulders, carrying enough force to halve the back of his skull. I slide the blade out of him, leaving only the skin of his face intact. His brain seeps out and is immediately squished beneath him. From somewhere deep within me, I feel something not unlike a smirk.

"What dark magic is this?" I ask, dodging a soldier with a spear. "I've not faced battle in twenty years. Never was I this skilled in combat. Never was I this pleased over such mutilation."

You're not fighting. This is where I take control.

Two soldiers thrust their spears at me. The first I swat away with my sword. The second is faster and plunges the tip of his blade through my hollow eye socket.

My sword drops. The chill leaves my body and I go limp. In my fading vision, I see the soldier begin to grin.

"I've failed already?" I say.

I think not.

The chill gladly returns and I grab the spear in one hand, the soldier's collar in the other. Twisting my head, the weapon snaps. I yank the man toward me and plunge the broken end of the spear through his eye. He falls back, writhing in agony, his head plucking the weapon from my skull. I rip the spear tip from his head, spinning it like a dagger in my hand. The other spearman approaches with another strike, but I swat away his attack and draw him closer. I stab him six times under the ribs, straight to his heart. I then throw the spear tip through the other soldier's remaining eyeball, silencing his screams.

At the chess table, the elf casually moves her knife and says, "Check," to her companion.

He rubs the scruff on his chin and says, "I'm not even thinking of the board. I can't believe you kicked that man in the coin purse."

The guard I'd tripped is back on his feet. He orders his remaining comrades to surround me. With their swords aimed and myself unarmed I can't help but feel a rush of fear.

You're already dead. They can't kill you

"But Butterscotch," I plead.

The whisper, the elf girl, allows them to strike. My body contorts, bending only slightly as I put my weight on one heel. All four swords plunge straight through me at once. Deep within, I feel the little mouse wince, followed by the warmth of her blood.

"No!" I scream in silence. My entire body trembles from the strike. I lean toward the nearest guard and punch him across the jaw. He stumbles toward another guard, his sword still through me.

"No! No! No! No! No!" I scream, kicking another soldier away. Of the two who have control of their weapons, they both begin to stab repeatedly, close to my heart. I lunge at one, wringing his throat. I bash my forehead against his nose and he flails, weakly cutting his blade along the side of my face. I keep squeezing down, choking the life from him. The other soldier stabs me through the side and then the back. The whisper's chill overwhelms me, forcing me to stop strangling the one guard. Against her will I jab him hard in the throat. I then turn to face my other attacker, feeling Butterscotch flop around inside my heart. I yank both swords from my body. "No! No! No! No! No!"

"What are you?" The soldier screams, trying for another strike. I cross my blades, forcing his toward the ground. I then step on it, letting it dig through my boot. His hands release the weapon as he backs away. With both swords I cut from his shoulders down through his hips. His viscera spills out both sides of him. I turn away, leaving him to gargle to death.

Two left.

"Three," I say.

The chill kicks my foot with the sword stuck in it. The blade dislodges and flies lightly, flopping in the air, stabbing straight into the soldier I'd left to choke on the ground.

Two.

Within me, Butterscotch stops thrashing and slows down.

One guard turns to run. I throw both swords. The first severs his shin, forcing him to fall forward. As he drops the other stabs through his ear.

The final soldier simply cowers. He backs closer to the gate, arms raised as though it might save him. Even if I would spare him, I already know the whisper will not. “Please,” he says. “I’ll do whatever you wish. I surrender. I’m defeated. You need not kill me.”

From the chess table the elf girl says, “It’d be best if you open the gate for him.”

The soldier nods as I pick up my sword. I approach him and he asks, “Is that what you want? You want through. I can let you through.” To the side of the gate, a chain has been run through the wall. A new addition, one I see meant to keep the inhabitants in rather than attackers out. The soldier pulls on it, raising the gate slightly. I see spikes have also been welded to the base. “See. Up with the gate. I wish no trouble.”

I stand beside him as he raises the gate, holding the chain steady. The chill runs through me and I grab the soldier by the shoulder, shoving him against the door frame. “It’s open! It’s open!” he screams. To which the chill makes me nod. I then punch him square on the nose. He stumbles. His head hits the frame and his hand releases the chain. The gate drops only a little, stopped by its own spike driving through the soldier’s skull. With the Fortian soldier wedging the gate open, I pass straight through.

Within my chest, I feel Butterscotch’s heart slowing, calming down.

Forgive me, the whisper says, and I turn back to the elf girl. Again she watches me, and I feel her voice within my head. *I tried to contort you so the blades wouldn’t pierce your heart, but one of the soldiers adjusted as you moved. I meant to be more careful.*

"Can you raise her?" I ask. "Necromancer?"

I can only manipulate the dead. But I feel the part of Butterscotch that died within you. I'm afraid to say her left ear has been severed down to a stump. The rest of her remains in tact. She will survive.

A pull on my cheeks may have formed a smile had my jaw not been removed. Within me I feel the scared mouse, rubbing a paw over the side of her head. Within her, several pups squirm.

At the chess table, I hear the hooded man sigh. "Very well," he says. "I owe you a cantaloupe."

I ascend another floor into the tower. The next level is the throne room, used for the village council and nobles to conduct kingdom business. At its center lies the seal. A magic emblem, fashioned to appear as the mink of my family crest, the amber seal is lined with stones crafted to protect the ruling family. Any intruder who steps beyond its border will instantly set ablaze.

Can you cross this horizon?

"If not the mice and I will perish," I say. I step to the ledge of the seal and the whisper's chill runs through my arm. My hand raises and reaches forward. As it goes over the seal, the azure flames appear from nothing and char my fingertips.

Failure. An utter waste.

"Release me," I tell the whisper. The chill dissipates and the flames cease. My arm drops limply to my side. "So. I may pass the seal. You cannot. Perhaps if you can push my body it'll land far enough to escape the magic's grasp."

What of Butterscotch?

"I remember when my brother had been infected with worms he still passed the seal without burning from the inside. The mice live within me. They are me. I do not fear for them as long as I make it to the far side."

If we fail, your kingdom falls to Fortia.

"I am an Ara. A protector of the earth. I will not fail."

The chill rolls through my legs and marches me back to the entrance.

I'll give you all the strength I can.

The chill pulses and I lunge forward in a sprint. I clutch my sword tight, charging forward. The seal is closer. Closer. I come upon its ledge, leap into the air, and-

Arise, Lector.

Arise, Lector.

"Am I a pile of ash?"

Arise Lector. Open your eyes.

I feel Butterscotch within me, licking her paws and rubbing her ear. She's fine. I'm fine. And I see no need to waste time. The chill fills me and I contort my way to a stance. "Tell your hooded friend he owes you two cantaloupes," I say.

I will.

"Do you know which chamber Hrathos sleeps in?"

I have a beacon of sorts. But you know the way better than I. It's easier if we work together.

I ascend the tower, my home, my sword dragging along the floor. To bring a weapon into these halls feels disgraceful. Disturbing. These were the rooms my father taught me to understand the stones in. These were the halls Clea and I danced through when we had first been wed. My brother and I played hide and seek around these corners. After we grew, the game continued with our children joining us. This castle, this tower was meant as a symbol of prosperity and community. Built at the peak of the highest mountain, it was a glorious beacon for all the world to look upon. Wealthy, happy, and virtuous. A gathering of men and dwarves, set in stones for a prosperous eternity. Not a place for arms. Never a place for shedding blood.

Within me I feel the whisper's sadness. *I used to have a home*, she says. *Until Fortia took it from me.*

"Is this why you raised me? For revenge against the pure kingdom?"

In part. A taste of revenge for myself although I know not how mine could ever be complete. You have my sympathy, Lord Lector Ara. I do hope your mountain continues to thrive long after this night.

I reach my family's bedchambers and see two Fortian guards standing post. Their deaths come faster than the soldiers from the courtyard, and are equally gruesome. As I pull my sword from the second one's body, I tell the whisper, "You seem to enjoy the flavor of revenge."

I hope you do the same. Understand though, this is happening whether you will it or not.

"I don't understand," I say, turning directly to my daughter's bedchamber.

You will.

I creek open the door. The embers of a flame long since extinguished still glow within the fireplace. I wish not to enter the room, but the chill pushes me onward. Immediately I see them together, intertwined. Alaila, more of a woman than I'd wish to know, lies draped over Hrathos. The butterscotch curls of her hair blanket his sweat sheened chest. Their hands are joined. My approach is slow, silent. "This old man?" I say. "He forced her. He used some magic against her."

Some magic. Some charm. Yes.

I feel the chill graze along my spine, but different from before. Warmer. Like daylight. It's as though the whisper is rubbing my back.

I can make this quick, Lector. I can take control and finish everything in a blink. But I want you to understand fully why you're there. You deserve as much.

"What do you mean?"

I feel something. Something else in that room is dead. My beacon. To your left.

I'm turned to my daughter's armoire.

Yes. In there.

The whisper and I both move forward. I open the armoire doors and stare at an arrangement of dresses.

Lower.

I crouch. Beneath the dresses are several pairs of glittering shoes. Next to them, a small black chest with silver trim. I pull it from the armoire, inspecting its design. The box was not fashioned by any hand in Ara. It seems unlike any work I'd seen from Fortia. Too crude. Poorly finished. Definitely human. No dwarf nor elf would allow a noble girl to possess such a thing.

It's from Fellen, a rogues' town on the northern continent.

"How do you know this?"

I purchased it in Fellen. With instructions to have it delivered to our client. Your daughter.

I'd have dropped the box had the whisper not sturdied my hand. "You gave this to Alaila?" I look to my little girl, asleep over a Fortian man. "What's in this chest?"

You know already. You know as well as me.

The chill runs through my other arm, trembling my hand. The lid comes off easy, and through the whisper I feel waves of warmth. Not the same as before. This is more distant. A memory. But not my own. It's of a fire pit at a woodland campsite. I see my daughter in a blue cloak, her lover in garments matching hers. She smiles like her mother as she says, "I'll be out of the country as well. For proof of death, I ask only that you deliver me his beard."

She hired my companion and I. We're the ones who saw to your demise.

The chill fills my entire body. It makes me look within the box. It makes me unfold the tattered handkerchief that envelops my jaw. "Impossible," I scream. How I try to scream.

It was any other job. An heiress wants her father dead for the fortune. Stage the accident. Leave him to rot and collect our reward.

"You killed me! You murdered me!"

My companion killed you. I only spoke to your daughter. Had we realized the man with her was a Stolzel, we'd likely have slaughtered them both.

"What is the meaning of this?" I fight against the chill, but am overpowered by its embrace. I cannot fight the necromancer's strength. "Why did you awaken me in my grave? Why do you torture me after you've already taken my life?"

The wedding, Lector. Think of the wedding.

The chill thrusts visions through my mind. My daughter, betrothed to this Fortian man. All my lands, all our riches being delivered to Fortia. He'll see to it. He'll give his king the wealth he needs to expand his kingdom. He'll spend my people's future to build an empire.

Your daughter acted as a diplomat, did she not? In foreign lands, she learned of the moon gods. She learned of a world outside your caves. A young woman, she rebelled against your ways. She is weak.

Malleable. Who do you think guided her mind? Who do you think gave her such confidence? Who taught her to live against your traditions?

Her words from the whisper's memory echo through me. "Deliver me his beard."

Foolish child. She probably thought she was saving your mountain. She couldn't know her crimes.

"Lies!" I scream. I writhe. "Lies! My own daughter would never do this. "She knows the punishment for those who turn against Ara." I don't know whether or not it's the whisper or I who picks up the sword. "It was this man! Hrathos! He seduced her."

My stirring awakens them. My daughter gasps and soon as Hrathos sits up I let my blade fly. The beginning of some word escapes his lips, but it doesn't matter. The blade pierces his mouth and continues straight through, stabbing into the headboard behind him. Blood sprays as his body slumps and falls from the bed. Everything above his jaw rests on the blade of the sword. His eyes are terrified, fixed on me. They tremble for a moment, wide and unblinking. Slowly they become still.

All the while my Alaila screams.

The chill fills my body. With no control I pounce over my daughter. With a ferocity I'd never known in life I grab her by the throat and urge her face close to the sword. Her arms flail until she grabs hold of my wrist. I leaned in, my eyes snarling. In my mind I continued to scream, "No! This cannot be true! She would not do this to her own father. Please, let me stop. Let me be dead again! Allow this madness to end!"

Within me Butterscotch claws at the walls of my heart. She'd had enough scares for one night and works to liberate herself from my body.

The whisper urges my daughter's head closer to the blade. "Please," Alaila begs. "You can have anything. Take anything. Please. It's all worth more than you'd ever need."

Bring her to the window.

I cannot resist the whisper's strength. With one hand I lift my daughter by the throat. I bring Alaila to the window of her bedchamber, leaning her outside so she can see the elf girl and her hooded companion below. They casually wave hello.

"No!" Alaila scrambles for something to cling to, some surfaces to connect with. "I'll pay them. I swear. I'll give them all they asked and more."

Too late. She must've thought herself invincible inside her little castle. Protected by her new family. When we sought payment she'd left us a satchel of bread and a letter declaring that it wasn't too late to devote our souls to the moons.

"No! Not my daughter! I cannot believe my own flesh would do this!"

I feel Butterscotch find her opening. The hole left from the sword that pierced my heart. She fights to scramble through it.

She will give your lands to Fortia. Your people. Your traditions. They will all be taken and forced to serve the pure kingdom.

The whisper raises my daughter higher and turns her to face me. "I'll pay them," she begs. "I swear."

From the whisper's memory I hear her say, "Deliver me his beard."

I try to resist. I try to fight the whisper's strength. "Please! Give me a moment. Let me show her the error of her ways. I can turn her around. I can stop her insanity. Please."

The girl killed her lord father for a kingdom she'd turn her back on. You said your grandparents didn't deserve to be remembered and she is no better.

"She's just a child! Barely a woman. You cannot force me through this!"

The whisper runs its chill through my free arm. I lower the shawl from over my face, revealing my exposed throat. The whisper lets her see what she purchased. And for that she stops struggling entirely. "Father," she whispers. "This moonless life. It's true. Look at how it corrupted your soul. Look at your heathen kingdom. The gods can save it."

"No," I say. Or want to say. She doesn't understand what she means. Alaila doesn't know how she betrayed Ara. I beg, "Please don't make me do this. I am not my father. I can forgive my blood for her mistakes. Please!"

In spite of all my love, all my resistance, the whisper clenches my fingers against Alaila's throat. The chill surges through my arm, and I watch as my daughter's trembling lips fade to blue.

Forgive me, Lector. Had she betrayed only us, I could allow you that chance. But we cannot risk Fortia gaining more power. You know their disease of purity. They'll claim your lands. In time they'll slaughter your people. Just like mine.

"Please. She will pay you. We will set this right."

This is for more than her life.

The whisper must feel the rage within me. The drive to kill the necromancer and her companion fills me as I feel the life weakly pulsing through my daughter's throat. Alaila goes limp. With a final squeeze the whisper shatters half the bones in her neck.

"I'll have your heads for this!" I scream. How I want to scream.

I think not.

The whisper sighs. Her chill leaves and both my daughter's corpse and mine crumble through the window. We fall like rotted apples from a tree and splatter against the hard face of the mountain.

Everything is still. As I drift back to nothingness I feel Butterscotch purge herself from my chest and sniff the night air. She looks around, shivers at the twilight, and catches the scent of my daughter's perfume. The little mouse is intrigued and scampers to Alaila's body. She prods at first with her paws, and then laps the blood off her skin. Taking delight at her fresh meal, the cave mouse takes her first bite of my daughter's face. From within, I feel her pups begin to stir.

###

The story of **Whisper** continues...

Necromantica

The Kingdom of Fortia faces an apocalypse. Orcs have invaded from the East, massacring their way straight to the holy city Dromn. While the kingdom makes its final stand, a mysterious necromancer elf and her human companion plunge through the battle in a high stakes mission to loot the king's palace. But with the city aflame and the battle stretching to every horizon, can they pull of the greatest heist ever? Can they even escape with their lives?

ROADSIDE ATTRACTION
PART ONE: SIREN NIGHT

Opening a monster series somewhere in the middle, Siren Night is a typical day in the life of Millie VanCastle. College drop out with telepathic abilities, as she drives her immortal, bigot boss, Gus, around the country on the hunt for the biggest and baddest monsters of all time. When Gus picks up on the trail of bones left by a trio of sirens along the Gulf of Mexico, the hunt takes him to a karaoke bar in Alabama. Millie gets dragged along for a night of strong drinks, bad singing, guns blazing, blood orgies, and vampire skin boots that sparkle in the daylight.

Tender Buttons Two:
Disco Wrecklord

In 1914, American writer Gertrude Stein published the original Tender Buttons, a masterpiece in verbal cubism. Today, we live in a world of unnecessary reboots and sequels. So it shouldn't come as any surprise that we proudly present Tender Buttons Two: Disco Wrecklord, in which famed poet and muse Gertrude Stein has taken the English language hostage. It's up to the grammar police of Scotland Yard to diffuse, edit, and clarify her madness before she conjugates run on sentences improper loop loop slipping away, away, away There is no there there.

BONNIE BEFORE THE BRAIN IMPLANTS

EXPONENTIAL INNOVATIONS: BOOK ONE

Exponential Innovation's newest employee is Bonnie Neman; one of the greatest mind's the world will ever know, a recent college graduate, and therefore qualified only for an entry level position. As an introduction to this sci-fi comedy series, Bonnie tours several labs in new her workplace, repeatedly discovering just how easy it is to reach out and touch the impossible.

About the Author

Keith Blenman hails from Metro Detroit where he teaches forensic analysis and works in a retail warehouse. He is short, chubby, and heavily tattooed.

OTHER BOOKS BY THIS AUTHOR

Please visit your favorite ebook retailer to discover other books by Keith Blenman:

The Vecris
Whisper: A prelude to Necromantica
Necromantica
Ferrelf (coming soon)

Roadside Attraction
Book One: Siren Night
Book Two: Tramp Stamp Vamp
Book Three: Ruff Stuff (coming soon)

Other fiction
Bartered Breath
Black Friday
Bonnie Before The Brain Implants
Braaaaaains
Entrees & Statistics
Tender Buttons Two: Disco Wrecklord
Where Dogs Sweat

ACKNOWLEDGEMENTS

Thank you Tom Budday, Christina Irwin, and Caroline Maun reading, criticism, and feedback.

Thank you again Christina Irwin for your amazing cover art.

Thank you again Tom for letting me use your poem at the beginning of this book.

Thanks to my parents, Jim and Joanne, and my four brothers, Mike, Josh, Dan, and Chris. Just because.

Connect with Keith Blenman

I hope you enjoyed my book. I love to connect with fans, readers, and critics alike, so please check out my social media sites. Reviews on Goodreads, Amazon, iTunes, and other retailers are also always appreciated.

Twitter: @keithblenman

Instagram: @blenmankeith

Facebook.
http://www.facebook.com/bluedonutbooks/

Subscribe to Keith's blog:
http://keithblenman.blogspot.com